THE USBORNE BOOK OF
EASY PIANO TUNES

Philip Hawthorn

Edited by Jenny Tyler and Anthony Marks

Designed by Philip Hawthorn and Kim Blundell

Illustrated by Kim Blundell

Original music and arrangements by Sharon Armstrong and Daniel Scott

Music engraving by Poco Ltd., Letchworth, Herts

Tunes in this book

About this book

This is a book of tunes which you can play on your piano or electronic keyboard. It will help you to improve your skill as a player, and also read and understand music better.

In this book there are folk songs, tunes from classical music and jazz tunes. Some you won't have heard before because they have been specially written. There are also tunes for two players.

The tunes get harder as you go through the book. The first tunes are ones you can play without moving the position of your hands. The tunes at the end are more difficult.

Some pieces of music contain symbols or words that you may not have seen before. Every time a new music symbol or word appears, it will be explained in a box at the foot of the page.

During the last 250 years there have been lots of amazing and curious pianos made, such as one that plays itself. You can find out about these on some of the pages in this book.

You can find out about composers, such as Beethoven, and their music. There are lots of interesting facts about the tunes in the book. There is also a section about piano records which you can listen to.

Sur le pont d'Avignon

This is a very old French tune. The title means "On the Bridge of Avignon".

French

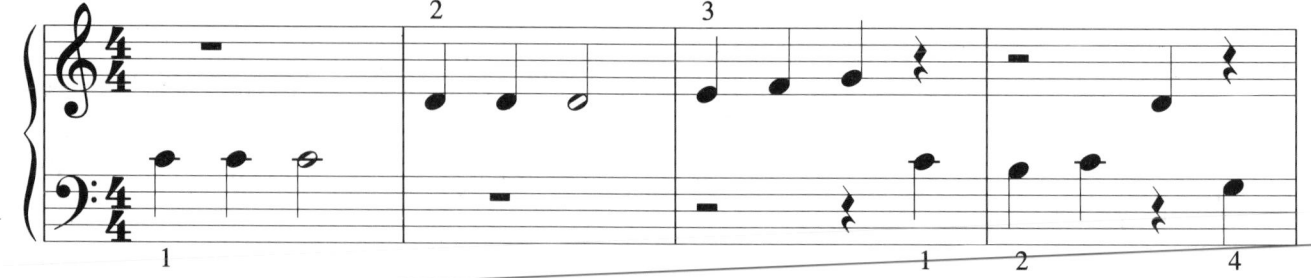

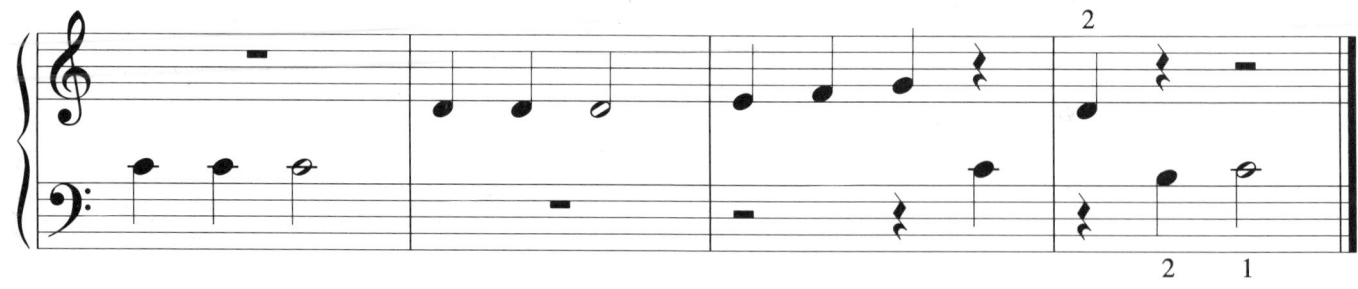

Note names

On the right is a picture to remind you of the names of the white notes on your keyboard, and where the notes are written on the music.

Right hand notes on this staff.

Left hand notes on this one.

This note is the C nearest to the middle of your keyboard. It is called middle C.

Finger numbers

Each tune in this book has numbers in it to tell you which fingers to use to play notes. This picture shows you which number stands for which finger.

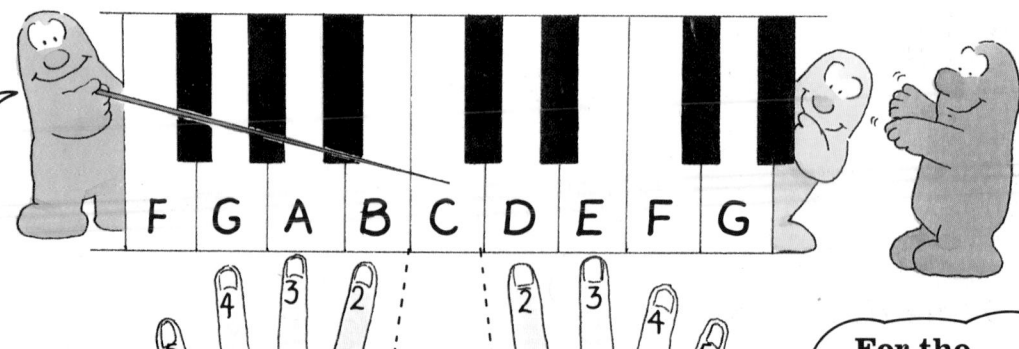

For the first few tunes in the book, you start with your thumbs on middle C.

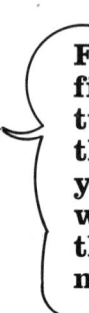

4

Yankee Doodle

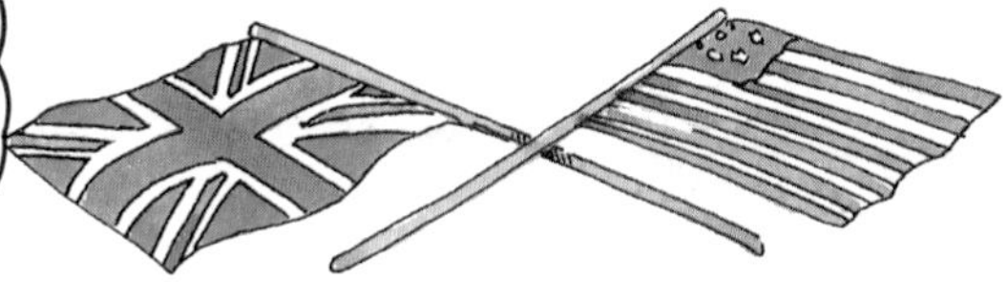

This song was written in America in the 1760s.

British soldiers sang it in the War of Independence.

American

Note lengths

Below you can see three types of note. Each one lasts for a different number of beats.

Semibreve (or whole note).* — 4 beats

Minim (or half note).* — 2 beats

Crotchet (or quarter note).* — 1 beat

Rests

When you see a rest on either staff, it tells you not to play with that hand for a certain number of beats. Below are three types of rest, with their lengths.

Semibreve rest (4 beats) **.

Minim rest (2 beats).

Crotchet rest (1 beat).

Time signatures

The numbers at the start of each tune are called the time signature. This tells you how many beats there are in each bar, and the length of the beats.

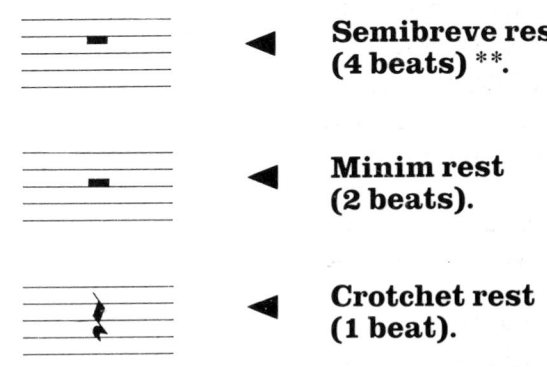

This number tells you that there are four beats in every bar.

This number tells you that the beats are crotchet length.

* *The names in brackets are what the notes are called in North America.*
** *This symbol is also used to show a whole bar rest of any number of beats.*

5

Bobby Shaftoe

Traditional

This is an English folk song, written in about 1760, about a man who goes to sea.

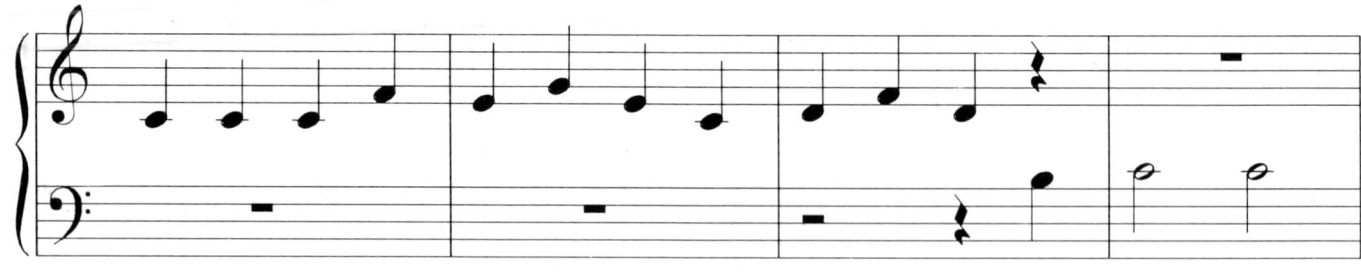

The first piano

The first piano was invented and built in 1710 by an Italian named Bartolomeo Cristofori.

It was called a "piano e forte" (which means "soft and loud" in Italian).

It could produce notes which were both soft and loud.

6

Row, row, row the boat

This tune has dotted minims in it. You can find out about them below.

Scottish

(musical score)

Dotted minims

A dot after a note increases its length by half as much again. A minim lasts for two beats, so a dot adds one beat to its length.

A minim is two beats long.

Half a minim is one beat.

A dotted minim is three beats.

This tune has two silent bars. For these, count three beats in your head.

7

On eagles' wings

There is another type of note in this tune. It is called a quaver.

Quavers

A quaver is half a beat long. Clap the rhythm on the right as you say the words. The quavers are the same length as each other, don't rush them.

Quick qua - ver claps

Quavers can be written on their own, like this.

8

The dinosaur and the dormouse

Some parts of this tune sound like a dinosaur, others like a dormouse.

I love rock music!

Amazing pianos

In the 1860s there were pianos which played themselves called pianolas, or player-pianos. There are some still around today.

This roll of paper has holes punched in it.

Look, no hands!

When these two pedals are pressed in turn, the roll moves round and the piano plays.

Two o'clock

In this tune, you have to play with both hands at the same time.

Keeping time

When you play music, you must keep a steady speed, or tempo. On the right are some ways of doing this.

These metronomes make a clicking sound to keep time.

You can alter the tempo to suit the music.

Most portable keyboards have built-in rhythms.

This tune was probably written in about 1650.

Girls and boys come out to play

There is a tied note in this tune. Find out more below.

English

Tying notes together

Notes on the same line or space can be tied together to make one long note. This has the same number of beats as the other ones added together.

This is called a tie.

3 beats + 2 beats = 5 beats

Do not play a new note in this bar.

11

 In this tune, you play one of the black notes on your piano. Find out more below.

Oh, dear, what can the matter be?

 This tune was written in Scotland around the year 1770.

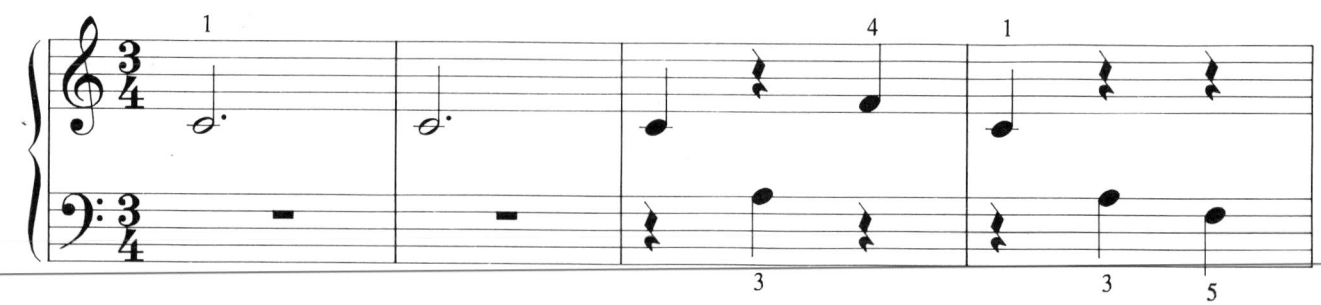

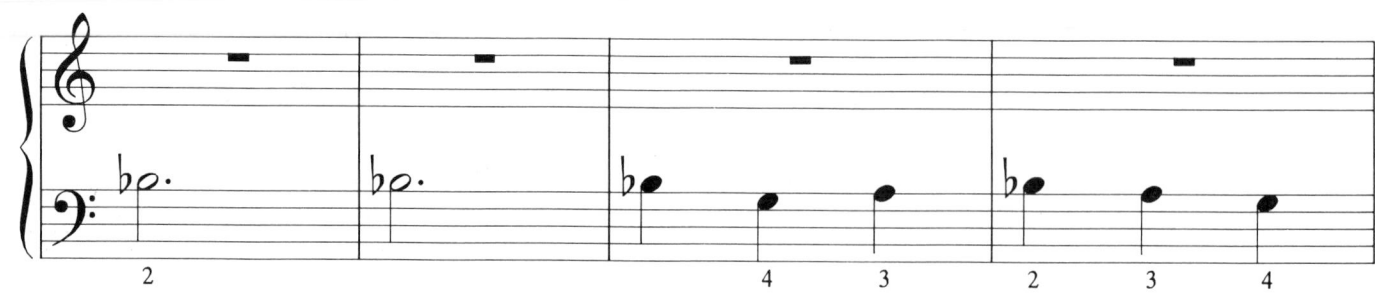

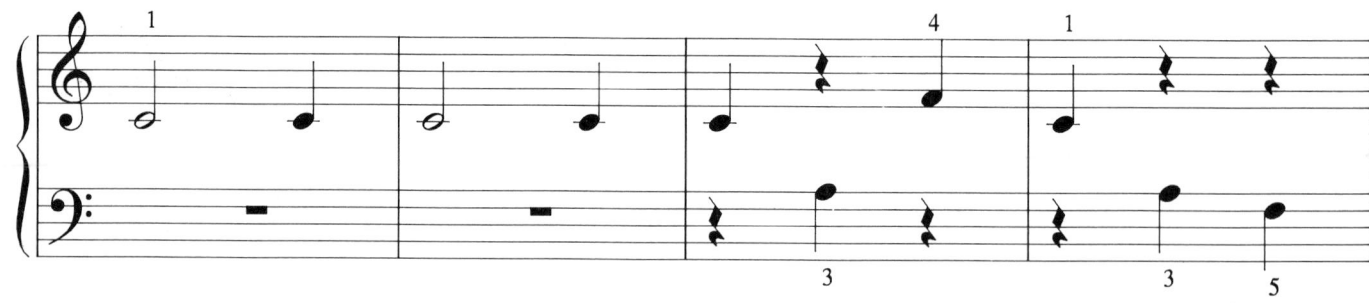

A black note

The black note in this tune is the one below B. It is called B flat. In the music, it has a ♭ sign in front of it.

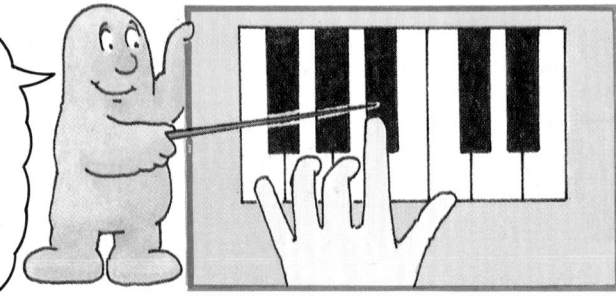 Before you play, put the second finger of your left hand on the B♭ note instead of the B note.

12

The bell ringers

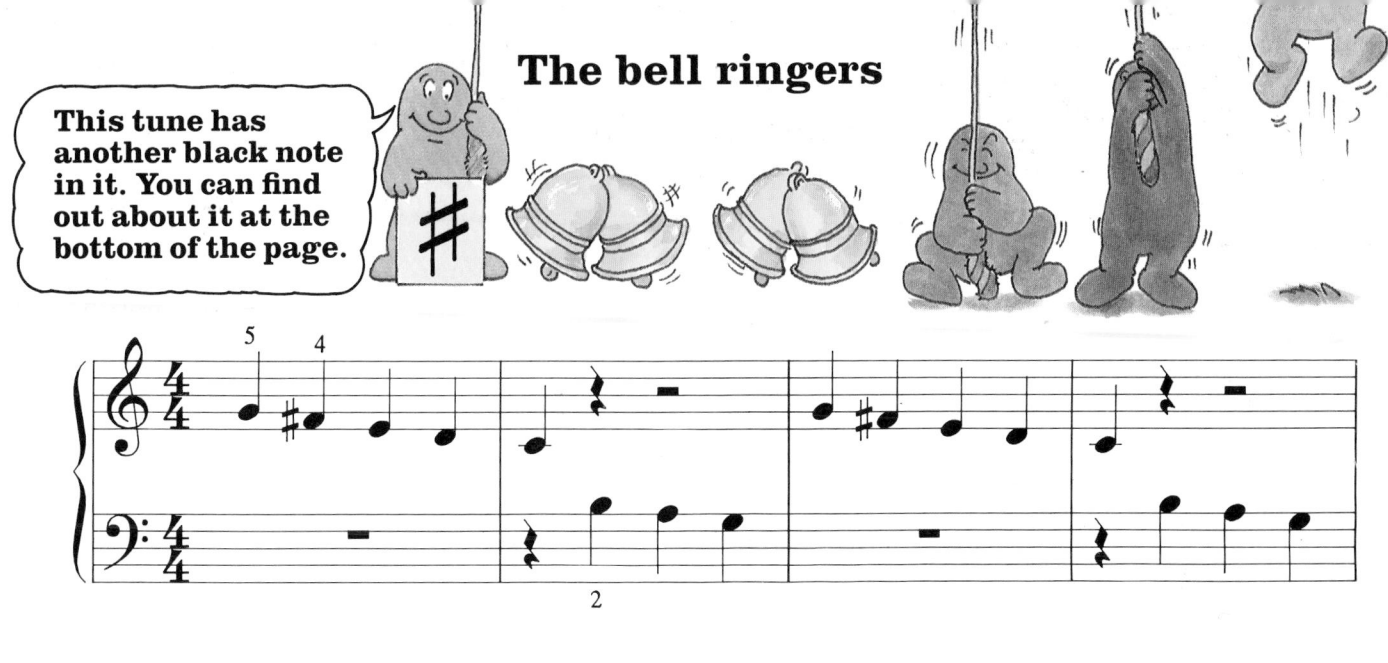

This tune has another black note in it. You can find out about it at the bottom of the page.

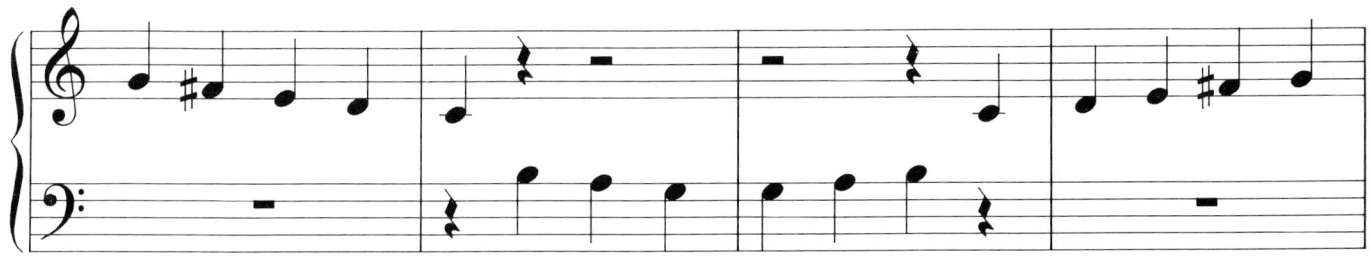

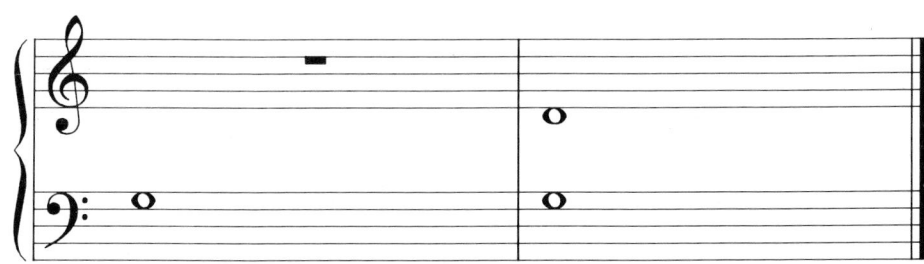

Another black note

The black note in this tune is called F sharp. It is the one above the F note and has a sharp sign, ♯, in front of it.

Put the fourth finger of your right hand on the F♯ note before you play.

Accidentals

A sharp or flat before a note is called an accidental. You play the note sharp or flat each time it appears in that bar. The barline cancels the accidental.

This sign is a natural. It also cancels sharps and flats.

13

Apache rain dance

When you play this tune, you will have to change your hand positions.

The finger numbers tell you where to move your hands.

Strings of notes

Sometimes you have to play lots of notes running up or down the keyboard. Here are two exercises for your right hand to help you to know which fingers to use.

Going up...

Start with your thumb on C and play the white notes using the 3-4-3 finger pattern above.

Thumb under finger.

14

Israeli folk dance

This tune starts with a bar of three beats instead of four. This is called a part bar.

Count a silent "one" in your head, then play the first beat on "two".

...Going down

Use these patterns all the way up or down the keyboard. Try and see.

Left hand

Use the right hand going up pattern for going down, and the going down one for going up.

5 4 3 2 1 * | 3 2 1 * | 4 3 2 1 * | 3 2

Start with your little finger (number five) on C and play the white notes using the 3-4-3 pattern above.

* **Finger over thumb.**

15

The tunes on these pages have letters to tell you how loudly or softly to play.

Ho-la-hi

The letters stand for Italian words. You can find out about them below.

German

Playing loudly

The words for loudness are based on the Italian word *forte* (for-tay) which means loud or strong. Press the keys firmly when you play *forte*.

ff

fortissimo means very loud.

f

forte means loud.

mf

mezzo (met-so) forte means quite loud.

16

How far is it to Bethlehem?

This tune has letters to tell you to play it softly.

There are more carols to play on pages 26-27.

Playing softly

The words telling you to play softly are based on the Italian word for "softly", *piano*. Press the keys gently to play *piano*.

mezzo piano means quite soft.

piano means soft.

pianissimo means very soft.

Haunted house

The notes in this tune have two sorts of dots. Find out what they mean below.

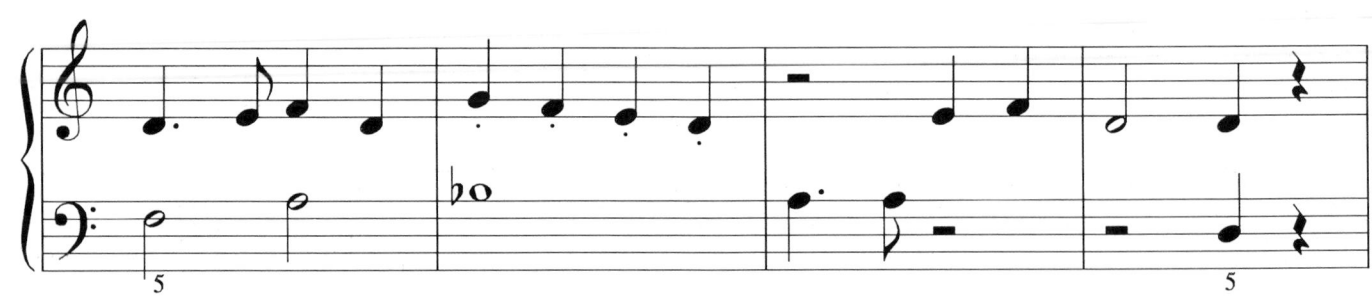

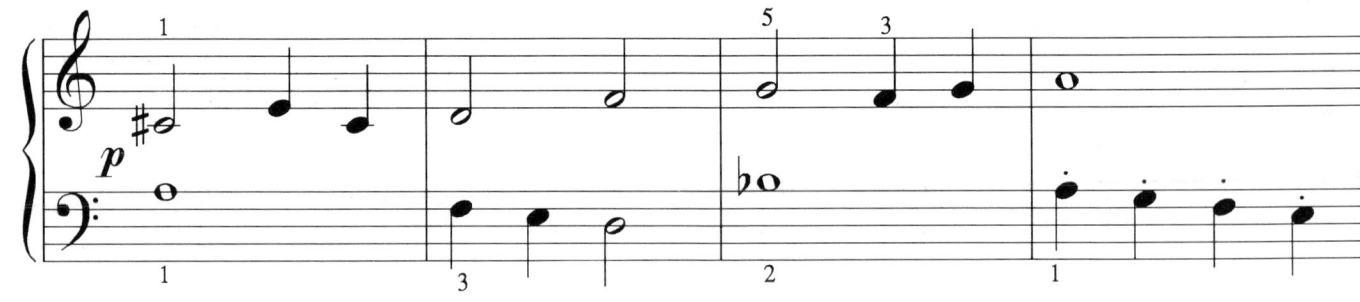

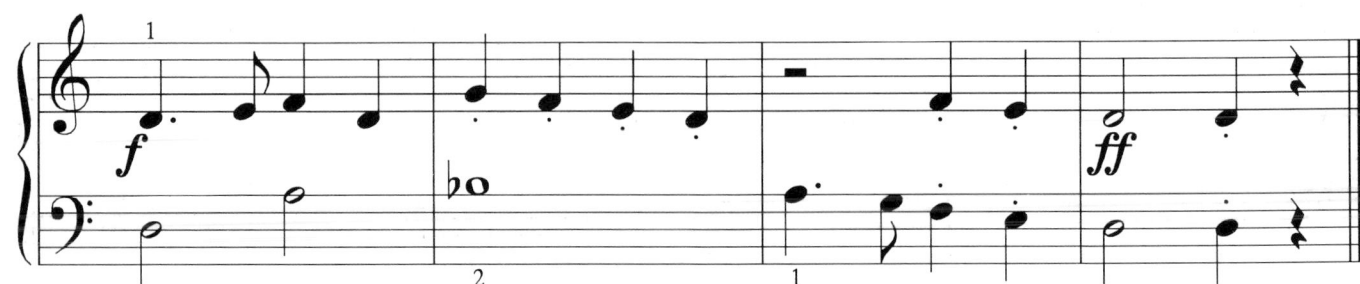

Dotted crotchets

A dotted crotchet is one and a half beats long. Here you can see how to play the right rhythm.

Clap on the beats that are underlined.

Playing staccato

When a note has a dot over or under it, play it short. Take your finger off quickly once you have played the note. This is called playing staccato.

18

At the fair

This tune is played very smoothly. Find out more below.

Playing legato

When notes on different lines or spaces are linked by a curved line, it means you play them very smoothly. This is called playing legato.

To play legato, press each note just before you take your finger off the previous one.

The notes linked by curved lines in this way are called phrases.

Where, oh where has my little dog gone?

English

This song, first sung in the late 1800s, was also known as "The Dutchman's Wee Dog."

Amazing pianos

These two pianos were shown at the 1851 Great Exhibition in London.

This "twin semi-cottage piano" was invented by John Champion Jones.

William Jenkin invented a piano for taking on ships. It collapsed to only 34cm deep.

20

Down in the valley

You have to play some of this tune twice. Find out more below.

There is an Italian word at the start of this tune telling you how fast to play.

Traditional

[Musical score: "Down in the valley", marked Allegro, 3/4 time]

How fast to play

Words written at the beginning of a tune tell you at what speed (tempo) you have to play it. Sometimes the words are Italian. This is because music was first printed in Italy. Below are some words to tell you different tempos.

Very fast
Presto

Fast
Allegro

Walking pace
Andante

Slowly
Lento

Repeating music from the beginning

The sign below is called a repeat mark. It means you go back to the beginning and play the tune again.

You only play the last bar of this tune once.

You ignore the repeat mark the second time.

The grand old duke of York

There are sharp signs at the start of this tune (see below).

English

Allegro

Key signatures

The ♯ written next to the clefs is called a key signature. You play F♯ instead of F all the way through the tune.

This tune is in the key of G major.

The key signature saves you writing a ♯ sign each time there is an F.

Remember, extra naturals, flats or sharps only apply to the bar in which they appear.

Lavender's blue

English

Two notes together

When you play more than one note at a time with one hand, it is called a chord. Here are some finger exercises to help you play chords more easily.

23

Anna's gerbils

Silent night

A teacher in Oberndorf school, Austria, wrote this tune in 1818.

The words were written by the Church's assistant minister.

Franz Gruber

26

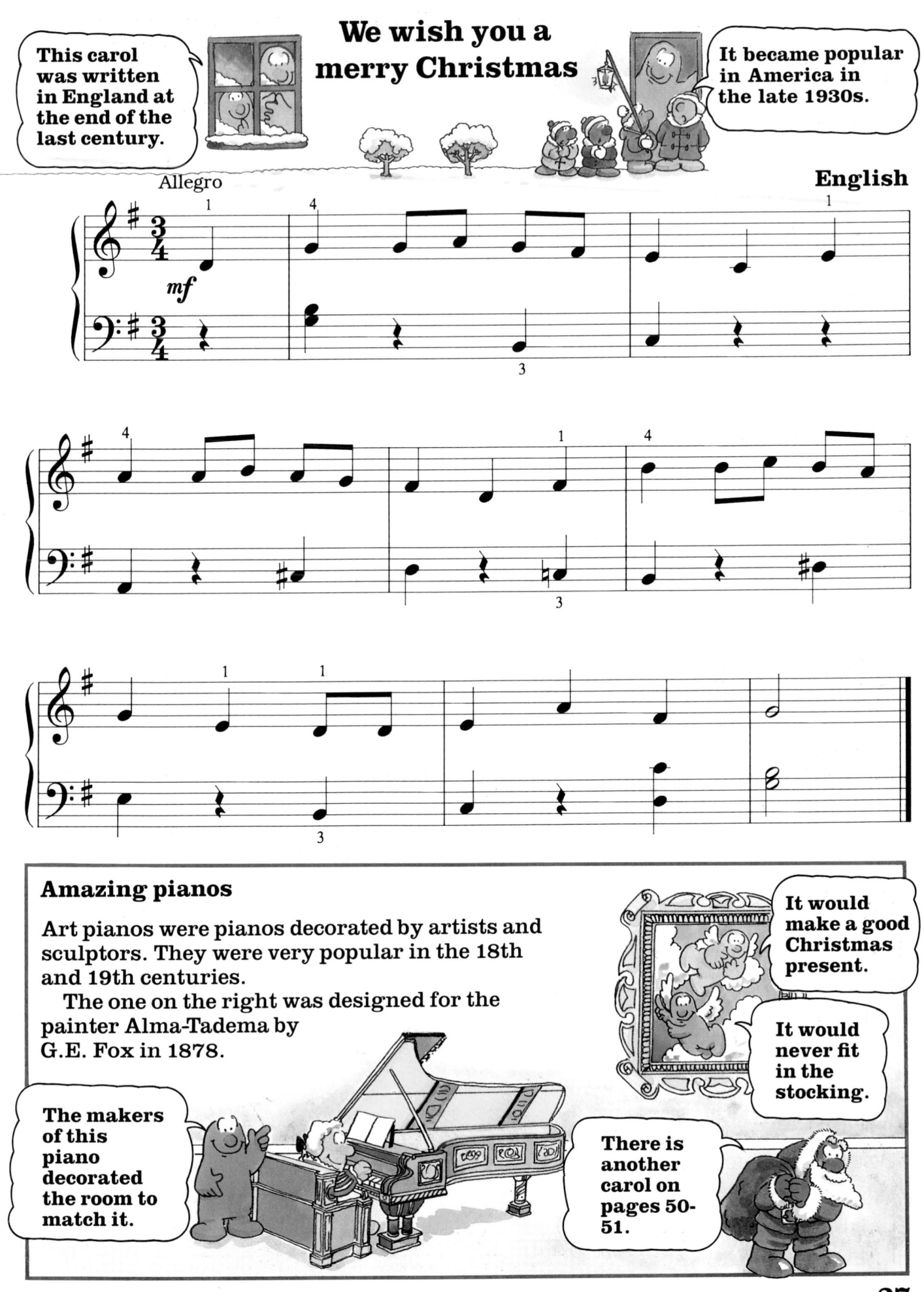

Burger bar blues

Blues began at the end of the last century. It was the folk music of black Americans.

There are two sets of repeat marks in this tune. Find out more below.

A set of repeat marks

On the right you can see what the second set of repeat marks in this tune mean.

This mark means "repeat from here".

Then repeat from the mark with the * on it.

The first time you get here, play the first time bar.

The second time, you skip this bar…

…and play this "second time" bar.

28

Space walk rag

Au clair de la lune

This tune was written by a French composer called Lully in about 1680.

The title is French. It means "by the light of the moon".

French

Amazing pianos

Johann Pape (1789 – 1875) had a piano factory in Paris. He built many unusual pianos. On the right are two which were strange shapes.

Frère Jacques

This tune is called a round. It can be played by two players.

The title is French for "Brother James".

French

A

mf

B

1 2 1

How to play a round

You can play this tune on your own, or you can play it as a "round" with a friend.

One of you starts playing from the beginning. When you get to the letter B, the second player starts from the beginning whilst the first continues to the end.

The first player starts playing on her own.

The second finishes playing on his own.

Two people playing on one keyboard

If two people play on one keyboard, this picture shows you which notes each of them could play.

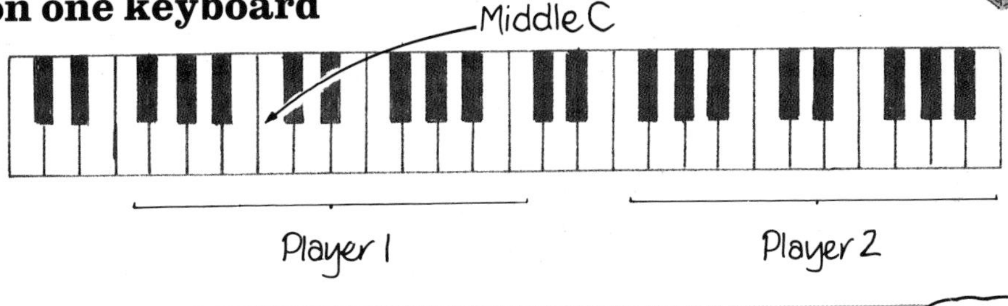

Middle C

Player 1   Player 2

Using a tape recorder

Instead of playing the round with two people, you could use a tape recorder and play both parts yourself.

First, record yourself playing the tune.

Next, play the tape back and join in on the piano when the tune gets to "B".

There is another tune for two players on pages 58-59.

31

Walking

This tune has three repeat marks. Look at the tune on page 28 to remind you what they mean.

Be careful not to confuse the tied notes with legato phrases.

Antonio Diabelli

More about phrases

Some music is written in phrases, like words are spoken in sentences. Lift your hand slightly after a phrase, before playing the next one. It is a bit like taking a breath.

When you speak, you can use questions and answers. It is the same with music.

The first phrase below is like a question which the second one answers.

Auld lang syne

Clementine

Dotted quavers

A dot after a quaver increases it by half as much again. Half a quaver is called a semiquaver. A dotted quaver lasts for three semiquavers.

Oh, Susannah

Stephen Foster

"From the New World"

Some parts of this tune get louder, and some get softer. Find out more below.

Dvořák was a Czech composer. He lived from 1841 to 1904.

Dvořák

Getting louder

This symbol between the staves means you get gradually louder as you play. It is called *crescendo* (cre-shen-do). Sometimes written *cresc.*

You start to get louder here.

You stop getting louder here.

The tune continues on the next page.

36

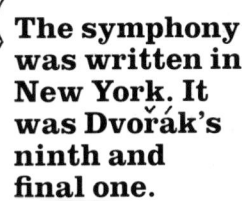
The symphony was written in New York. It was Dvořák's ninth and final one.

At that time, many Europeans thought of America as a "new world".

Parts of the music are based on American Indian folk music, spirituals and rags.

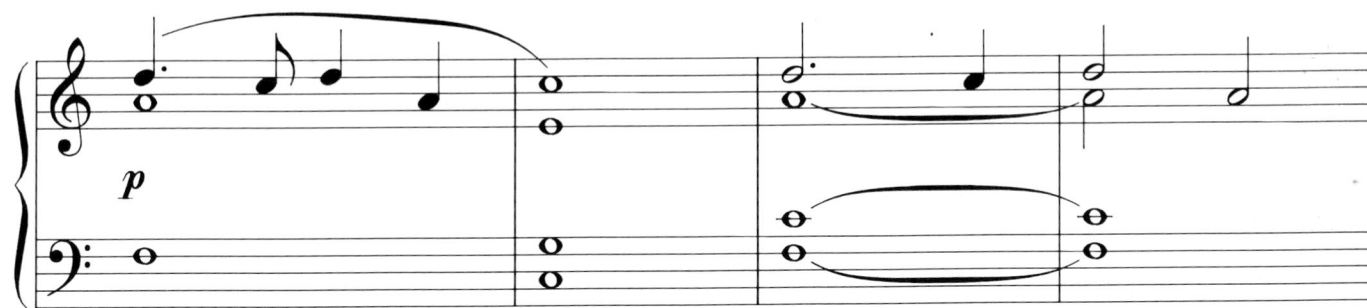

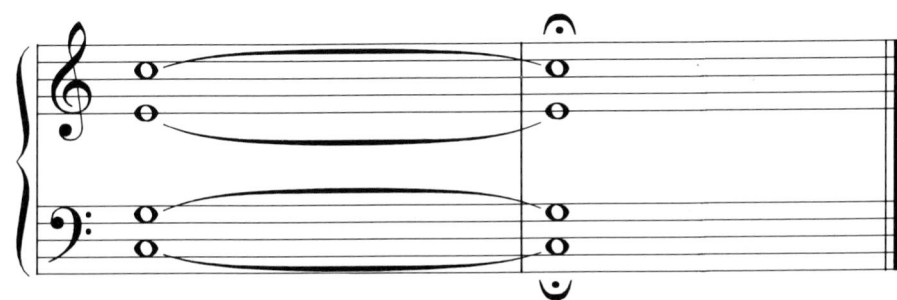

Getting softer

This symbol tells you to play gradually more softly. It is called *diminuendo* (dim-in-u-en-do). It is sometimes written as *dim*.

Remembering the symbols

To remember what each symbol means, look at the gap between the lines.

Gap getting bigger means get louder.

Gap getting smaller means get softer.

It's like turning the volume up or down.

Autumn

This tune is in 6/8 time. There are six quavers to each bar, in two groups of three.

Cantabile means "in a flowing style". It is Italian for "singing".

38

Winter

This tune has notes written on extra lines below the staff, called ledger lines.

There are tunes for the other two seasons on the next page.

Ledger lines

Ledger lines can be written above or below either staff. These are the ledger line notes in this piece:

Below the bass clef: B   A   G   F

Below the treble clef: E   D

The notes below the treble clef could be written in the bass clef. But they are written this way to tell you to play them with your right hand.

39

Summer

There are new ledger line notes in this tune. Find out more below.

More ledger line notes

In this piece there are two ledger line notes above the right hand staff and two above the left hand staff.

B A

D E

Remember, key signatures and accidentals also apply to notes on ledger lines.

Wedding march

Mendelssohn

This tune was written by a German composer called Mendelssohn. It is often played at weddings.

You have to repeat part of this tune. Find out more below.

Fine

D.C. al Fine

A new kind of repeat

Fine ("fee-nay") is Italian for "the end". *D.C.* stands for *Da Capo. Da Capo al Fine* means play from the top until you reach the *Fine* sign.

Start at the beginning and play through the piece once until you reach *D.C. al Fine.*

Then start again and play through to the *Fine* sign.

The thick barline shows you where to stop.

42

Daisy Bell

This tune is about a couple being married and going away on a tandem.

Harry Dacre

Nobody knows the trouble I've seen

Traditional

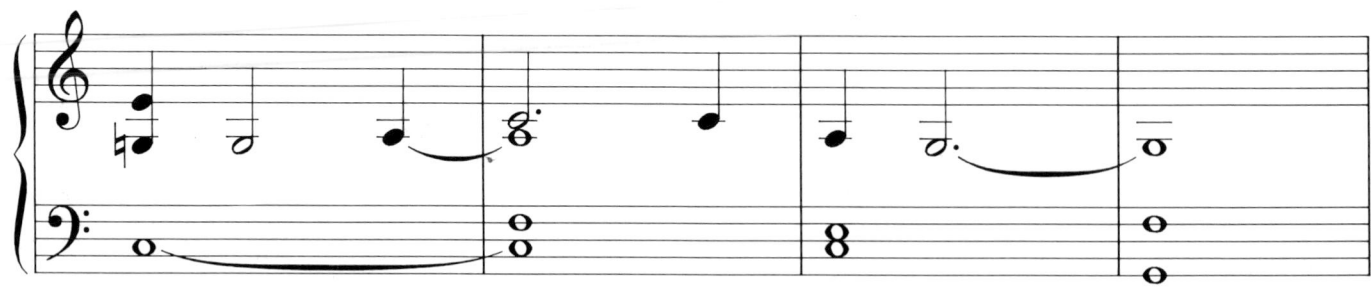

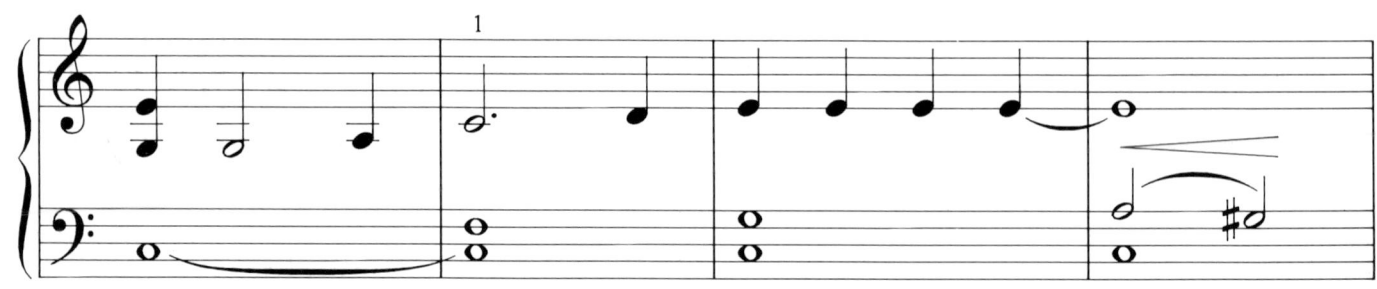

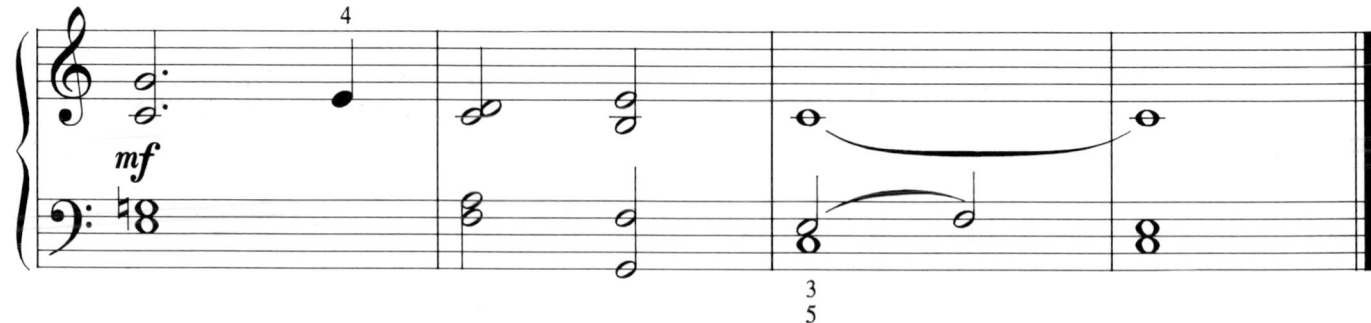

Spirituals

Spirituals were first sung in America in the middle of the last century. They were usually sung by black slaves.

44

Kum by yah

This tune is another spiritual.

The title means "come by here".

Traditional

Amazing pianos

In 1866 a piano was invented by a man called Millward. As well as the keyboard, it also contained a sofa, a desk, a mirror, lots of drawers, a wash basin, a sewing box, a writing table and cupboards for soap, towels, shaving equipment and bedclothes.

It might have looked something like this.

45

Riding on a donkey

Allegretto means "play not quite as fast as allegro".

This tune has notes with accents. Find out more below.

Traditional

Accents

An accent tells you to play the note by pressing harder and more quickly than usual.

How quickly you press a note is called the attack.

Accent notes are louder than normal.

Remember, this note is a semiquaver.

The rhythm on the left is twice as fast as the one on the right.

46

Toreador's song

This tune is from an opera called "Carmen", set in Spain. A toreador is a bullfighter.

Bizet was a French composer. He lived from 1838 to 1875.

Bizet

Allegro

Opera

An opera is like a play except that nearly all the words are sung.

There is an orchestra in front of the stage to play the music.

Operas were first written about the year 1600. Some composers who have written opera are Gluck, Wagner, Verdi and Mozart.

From the "Surprise" Symphony

Haydn

St Anthony Chorale

Haydn

We three kings

J. H. Hopkins

Pause When you see this sign over a note, you hold the note for a little longer than usual.

Lullaby

Brahms

52

Melody in A minor
(part A)

You play some of the music on this page an octave higher than it is written (see page 59).

Watch out! On this page both hands play in the treble clef.

61

Music help

On this page you can see all the music symbols, words and theory that are in the book. The index on page 64 will show where in the book they are explained.

Key signatures and scales

On the right you can see the key signatures used in this book. The key signature also shows you which sharps and flats are in that particular scale. For example, in the scale of G major (which begins and ends on G) there is an F♯.

C major

This is the same key signature as A minor.

G major

F major

D major

B♭ major

How fast to play

Here are the Italian words which tell you how quickly to play music.

presto	very fast
allegro	fast
allegretto	not too fast
andante	quite fast
lento	slow
ritardando	slowing down
a tempo	return to original speed
cantabile	in a flowing style

How loudly to play

The list below is to remind you about the symbols which tell you how loudly to play.

pp	very softly
p	softly
mp	quite softly
mf	quite loudly
f	loudly
ff	very loudly
crescendo	getting louder
diminuendo	getting softer

You can find out about these on pages 16 and 17.

...and these on pages 36 and 37.

Music symbols

Here are the symbols written in the music which tell you to do something.

pause		octave
emphasis		dotted
accent		staccato
repeats		grace notes
spread chord		slur
		tie

Ledger lines

These staves show you what note names different ledger lines have.

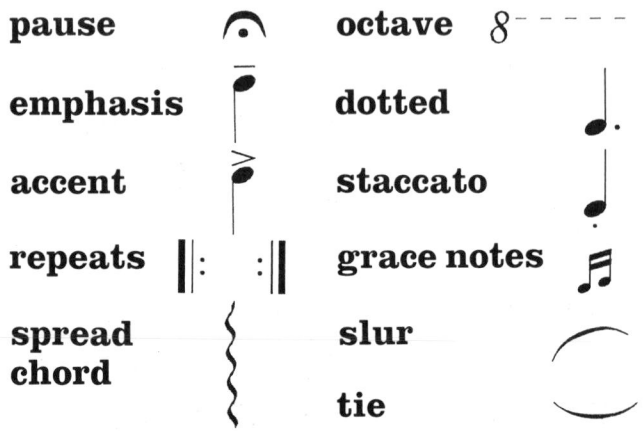

62

Listening to piano music

Here you can find out about classical and jazz piano music and some famous pianists.

Classical piano pieces

Below are some interesting piano pieces you can find on record, cassette or compact disc.

Bach	Preludes and Fugues
Beethoven	Concerto no. 5 in E flat
	Piano sonatas: "Moonlight", "Appassionata", "Pathétique"
Brahms	Piano Concerto no. 2
Chopin	Waltzes, Etudes, Nocturnes and Polonaises
Debussy	Children's Corner Suite
Gershwin	Piano Concerto in F
Grieg	Piano Concerto in A minor
Joplin	Rags (including "The Entertainer", "Maple Leaf Rag")
Liszt	"Consolation" in D♭
Mozart	Piano Concertos nos. 21, 22 and 23
	Sonata in A major
Rachmaninov	Prelude in C♯ minor
Satie	"Trois Gymnopedies"
Schubert	Piano Quintet in A major ("The Trout")
Schumann	Scenes from Childhood
Tchaikovsky	Piano Concerto no. 1

Classical pianists

Below are the names of some of the best known modern pianists. They have recorded a lot of music, including many of the pieces on the left.

Peter Donohoe
Artur Rubinstein
Vladimir Horowitz
Clifford Curzon
Vladimir Ashkenazy
Daniel Barenboim
Moura Lympany

Jazz pianists

Below are the names of some jazz pianists. They have made many recordings. Most of them have had their own bands. They each play music in their own style.

Jelly Roll Morton
Oscar Peterson
'Fats' Waller
Duke Ellington
Dave Brubeck
Chick Corea
Keith Jarrett

Amazing piano music

A musician named Czerny arranged a piece of music for eight pianos and 16 players.

The longest piano piece is called "The Well Tuned Piano" by La Monte Young. It is nearly four and a half hours long.

In another piece by La Monte Young, there was a music instruction to feed the piano on hay and water before playing it.

Index

This edition published in 1993 by Usborne Publishing Ltd, 83-85 Saffron Hill, London EC1N 8RT, England. Based on a previous edition first published in 1989. Copyright © 1993 Usborne Publishing Ltd.

The name Usborne and the device are Trade Marks of Usborne